MONSIEUR LAPIN

Plays Hide and Seek

Other books in this series

Monsieur Lapin in Hospital

MONSIEUR LAPIN

Plays Hide and Seek

Rhona R. McMillan

Illustrations by Joel Tuckera

ISBN: 9798401149107

PublishNation
www.publishnation.co.uk

Mon ami my friend beside me
is called Old Grumpy Ted.
He is not filled with joie de vivre,
he wears a frown instead.

He knows nothing of the joys of life,
his days are all the same.
What day is it? I'll work it out
with an elimination game.

Today, it isn't lundi Monday
as Sophie's school bag is on the chair.
Nor is it mardi Tuesday,
because her P.E. kit is here.

It can't possibly be mercredi Wednesday
as her clarinet is on the shelf
and if it was jeudi Thursday
she'd have made her bed herself.

Week in, week out, without a doubt,
her routine stays the same.
Today it can't be vendredi Friday
as her friend Jane never came.

If it was dimanche Sunday
we'd both be off to church.
She always takes me with her,
wouldn't leave me in the lurch.

So today **must** be samedi Saturday.
Hooray for something new!
I never know what to expect,
where we'll go, or what we'll do.

Quand il fait beau when the weather's nice
we might picnic in the park,
but quand il pleut when it rains,
we watch a movie in the dark.

Today the sun is shining.
We're sure to be outside:
the park, the beach, a woodland walk,
perhaps a long bike ride.

Le petit déjeuner breakfast is over
and very soon I'll know
just what the day has in store
and where we're bound to go.

Sophie scurries round the bedroom.
I'm watching for a clue.
She doesn't give me any hint.
She's looking for her shoe.

Sa mère her mother is at the door.
Is that a shopping bag I see?
I hope we're not going shopping,
that's such a bore for me.

At last, it seems we're ready.
Sophie lifts me off the stool.
I leave behind Old Grumpy Ted
who just sits there as a rule.

Sophie puts me in her basket
as we walk along the street.
There's a fierce dog in the neighbourhood
we do not want to meet.

Now we're waiting at the bus stop,
we must be going into town.
Wish they'd left me with Old Grumpy Ted
on the stool with his head bowed down.

A little girl pokes and strokes my ear
whilst we're standing in the queue.
I'm glad when we move forward
and we board bus forty-two.

I study people's faces
as we sit down on the seat.
Many look through la fenêtre the window
as the bus moves along la rue the street.

No-one happy, no-one smiling,
all just staring into space.
There's a sadness, or a worried look
on each and every visage face.

Quelle heure est-il? What time is it?
This journey's been quite long.
The bus has stopped, we're getting off.
I hear music and a song.

There is clapping. There is laughter.
There is talking and shouting aussi too.
So many people in a crowd
and pushing their way through.

In the chaos, Sophie drops me.
I am lying on the ground.
I watch her and she keeps on walking.
Please, Sophie, turn around!

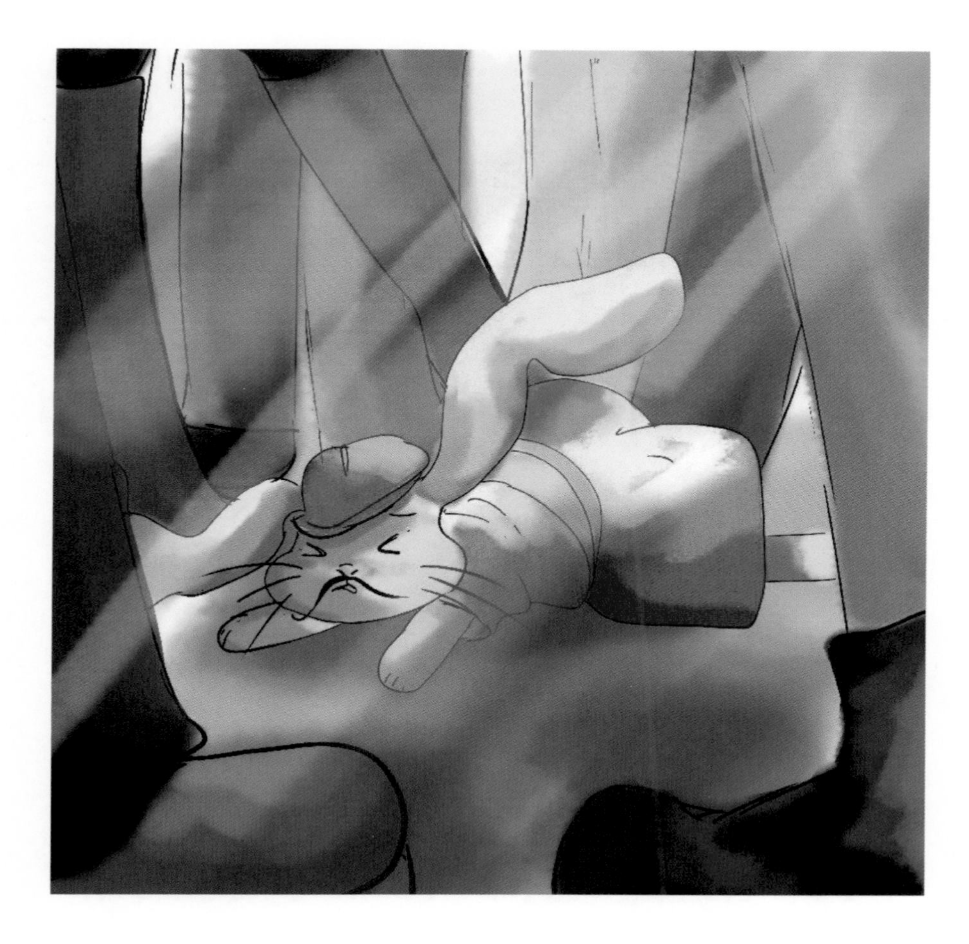

Helpless, I am lying here,
getting kicked and stood upon
by feet that hurry onwards
and, like Sophie, are soon gone.

I feel a wet sensation
and I hear a snuffling sound.
There is quelquechose something near me,
something furry, white, and round.

What a cute little fellow.
A tiny, friendly dog.
He nudges me and licks me,
hopping around me like a frog.

I think he wants to play with me.
He strokes me with his paws.
He rolls me onto my tummy
and gently lifts me in his jaws.

We're off, zig-zagging through the crowd,
between long legs and short.
My new friend and I bound along.
I hope we don't get caught.

Le chien the dog takes me to his master.
He's a trader in the street.
He stands still before him
and drops me at his feet.

"What have you brought me, Jacko?
Have you found un jouet a toy?"
He picks me up and throws me.
"Go fetch! That's a boy."

He has a powerful throw.
I'm whizzing through the air!
I knock a man's cap to the ground
while people stop and stare.

I land upon a cheese display,
between camembert and brie.
There are many more French cheeses,
but I don't get time to see.

"Excusez-moi" "Excuse me."
From the cheeses I am plucked
by a woman behind the counter
and into son sac her bag I'm tucked.

She's a seller of French cheeses.
"Roquefort et Comté," she cries.
Her Parisian accent obvious.
Time for me to exercise.

I must escape from mademoiselle,
this woman selling fromage cheese.
Rien Nothing can stop me moving.
"Excusez-moi, if you please."

The French that she has spoken
is all I need to hear.
I see Jacko in the distance.
My path to him is clear.

Jacko barks an excited greeting
when he sees me on my feet.
He turns and races swiftly,
disappearing down the street.

I'm dashing after Jacko
as fast as I can go.
That little dog's a sprinter
and I'm a little slow.

Hooray! I'm sure I spy him.
From behind une boîte a box I peek.
He's panting near a plant stall.
We're playing hide and seek!

He’s gone! I cannot see him,
so I begin to run.
I wonder where he’s hiding.
This really is such fun!

All around me fruit and veg for sale.
What a shopper’s paradise!
Champignons mushrooms, poireaux leeks
and varieties of spice.

The market place is busy.
There is a scuffle to my right.
There's a dog fight in the alley.
Then BANG! What a terrible fright!

I've collided with a dustbin.
I am dirty and I'm dazed.
I lie in a heap in the gutter,
my floppy ears battered and grazed.

A French voice is calling loudly,
"Pommes et pêches!" "Apples and peaches!"
Then stretching out towards me,
a familiar hand suddenly reaches.

How marvellous! Sophie has found me.
I just can't believe my luck.
Jacko is frantically pacing around
the dustbin that I struck.

How pleased I am to see them,
Sophie and her mum.
We're standing at the bus stop
waiting for l'autobus the bus to come.

Jacko's playground is the market place
where he is free to roam.
We shared a great adventure,
but now I'm heading home.

I live at home with Sophie.
I haven't got a care.
As long as we're together
it doesn't matter où where.

Où habitez-vous?
Where do you live?

Je suis content.
I am happy.

Printed in Great Britain
by Amazon

75266131R00022